The Rela

MW00488688

Story by Jenny Giles

Illustrations by Rachel Tonkin

Rigby

A Harcourt Achieve Imprint

www.Rigby.com

1-800-531-5015

"Look at the big children
over there," said Kylie.
"Can we have a race
like that, Miss Bell?"

"I'm sorry," said Miss Bell. "The big children are running relay races all day."

Then Miss Bell said,

"You can have

a little relay race

over here if you like."

"Yes!" shouted the children.

Zoë saw two batons

on the grass.

"We can have a red team

and a blue team," she said.

"Run around the tree
with the baton,"
said Miss Bell.
"Then come back,
hand off the baton,
and sit down
at the back of the line."

The children looked
at the first two runners.

"Get ready . . . GO!"
said Miss Bell.

The children ran fast.

They raced
around the trees
and came back again.

"Don't forget to hand
off the batons,"
said Miss Bell.

Zoë and Kylie
were the last two runners.
Kylie got the baton first
and raced away with it.

On the way back,
it fell out of her hand.

"Get the baton, Kylie!"
shouted the children
in the red team.
"Here comes Zoë!"

Kylie stopped to get
the baton.

"Run, Kylie! Run!"
shouted the red team.

"Go, Zoë!"

shouted the blue team.

Kylie and Zoë ran very fast.

They raced to sit down
at the back of the line.

"Who won, Miss Bell?"

shouted the children.

"Who won?"

"You all ran a good race," said Miss Bell.

"It was a **tie**!"